DC SUPER-PETS!™

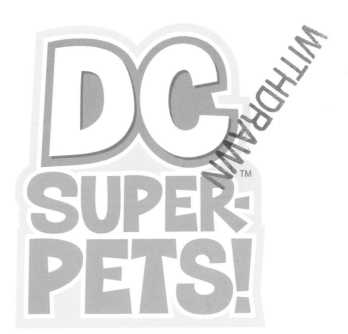

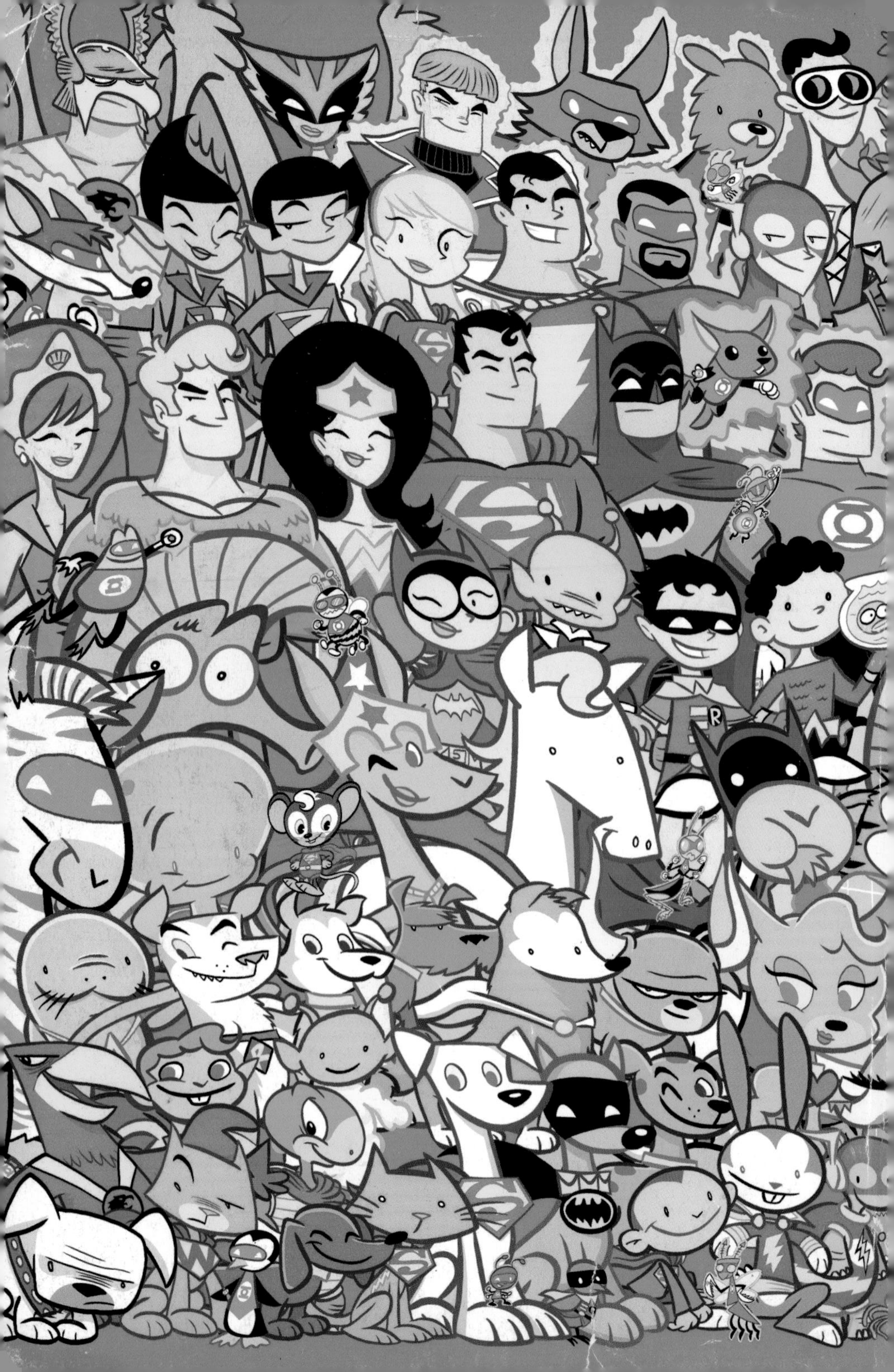

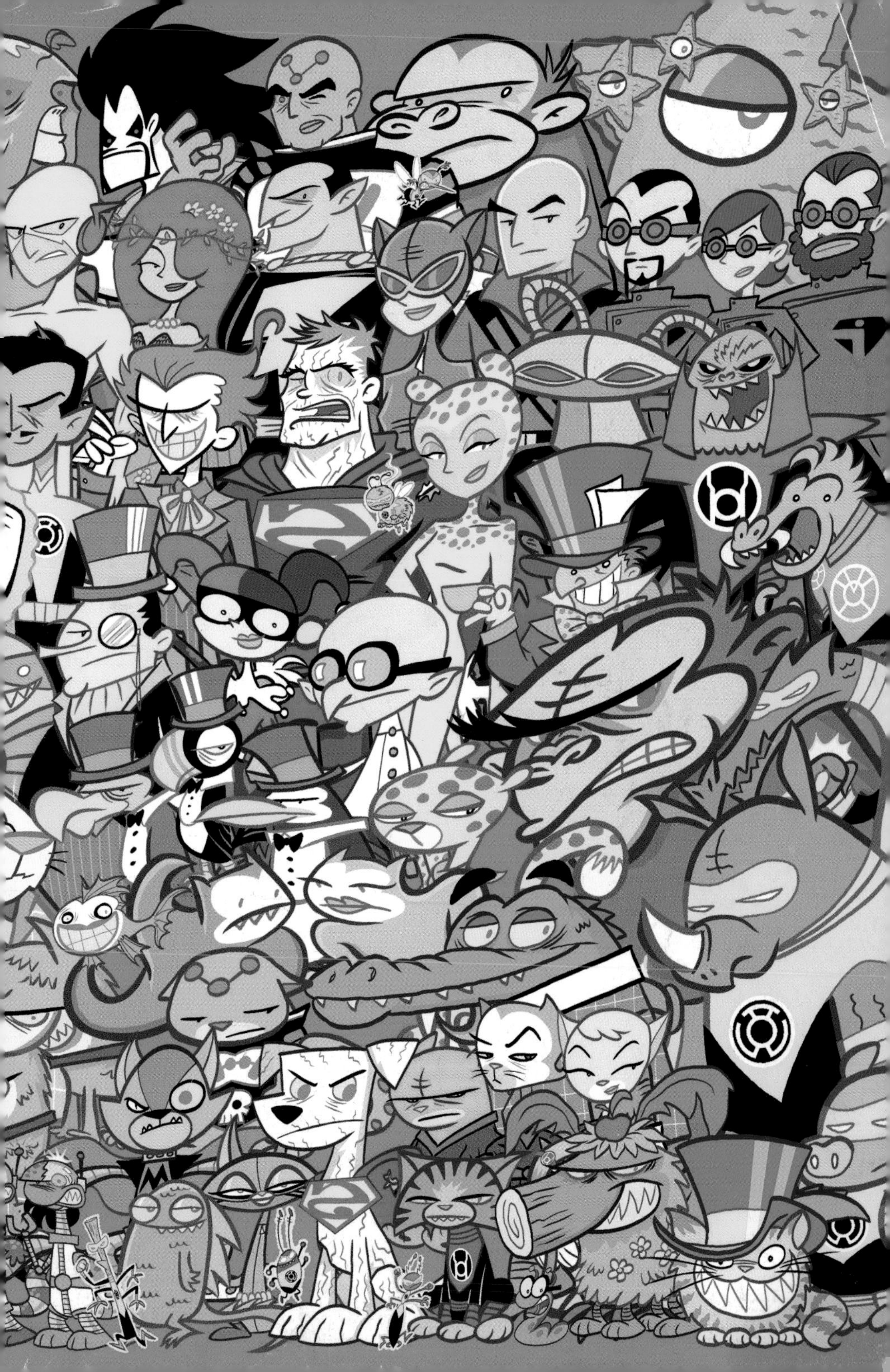

DC SUPER-PETS!™

by John
Sazaklis

CANDY STORE
CAPER

illustrated by
Art Baltazar

Batman created by Bob Kane

PICTURE WINDOW BOOKS
a capstone imprint

Starring...

ACE
THE BAT-HOUND!

ROBIN ROBIN
THE BIRD WONDER!

CRACKERS & GIGGLES
THE JOKER'S HYENAS!

ROBIN
THE BOY WONDER!

THE JOKER!

HARLEY QUINN!

TABLE OF CONTENTS!

SUPER-PET HERO FILE 014:
ROBIN ROBIN

Flight

High-tech Mask

Robin Logo & Secret Weapon

Utility Belt

Super Hero Owner:
ROBIN
(TIM DRAKE)

Species: American Robin
Place of Birth: Gotham
Age: Unknown
Favorite Food: Worms

Bio: Tim Drake trained his pet bird in the art of catching nightcrawlers and named the high-flying hero Robin Robin!

Super-Pet Enemy File 014:
CRACKERS

Funny Bone ——————

Wicked Grin ——————

Evil Heart ——————

Super-villain Owner:
THE JOKER

Super-Pet Enemy File 014B:
GIGGLES

Funny Bone ——————

Wicked Grin ——————

Evil Heart ——————

Super-villain Owner:
HARLEY QUINN

Chapter 1

WORLD OF WONDER

One Saturday morning, billionaire Bruce Wayne was away on business. His young friend, **Tim Drake,** was eating cereal in front of the TV at Wayne Manor. On the couch next to him was Bruce's dog, **Ace. Robin Robin,** Tim's pet bird, landed on his shoulder.

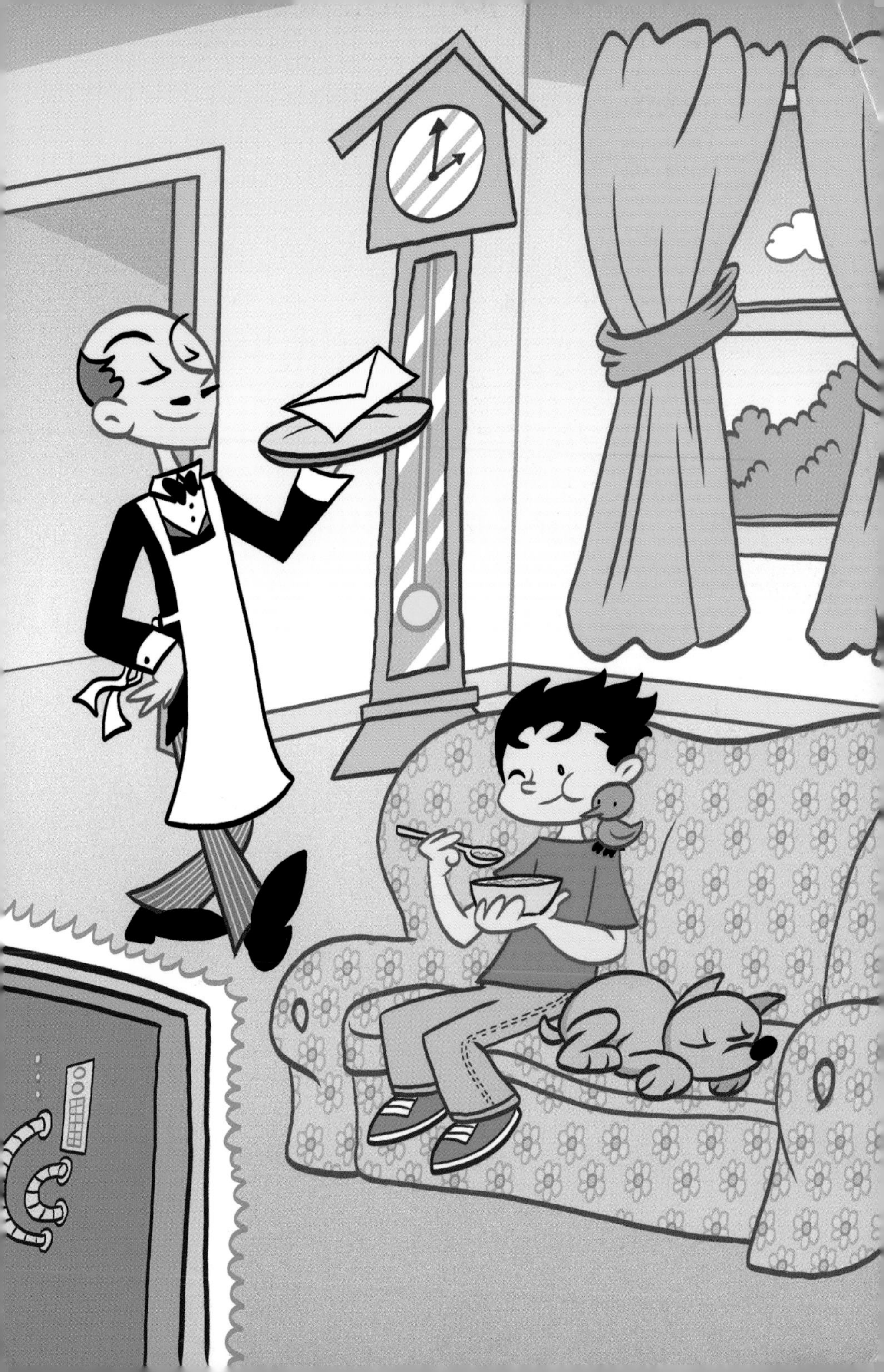

Just as the morning cartoons began, Alfred walked in. He carried a fancy invitation on a silver serving tray. "Master Tim, this came for you in the mail," the loyal butler stated.

Tim opened the glittery invite.

Dear Master Timothy Drake,

You are invited to a party at GRANNY GLEE'S WONDERFUL WORLD OF WONDER!

Doors open at NOON TODAY!

GRANNY GLEE

Under the fancy writing was a photograph of a smiling old woman. Granny Glee was opening a new store! It was part fun house, part toy store, and full of games and candy.

Tim leaped to his feet. Ace awoke, and Robin Robin flew to his perch.

"This is so cool!" Tim cried. "Alfred, can you give me a ride, please?"

"Certainly, Master Tim," replied the butler. "Once you've finished your breakfast, of course."

"Of course," Tim repeated, shoveling cereal into his mouth.

Meanwhile, Robin Robin landed on the invitation. Studying it closer, the little robin noticed something strange about Granny Glee. Under her pink polka-dot cap, she had big eyes and an evil grin full of sharp teeth. Plus, her skin was green and fuzzy!

"Ace, come quick!" Robin Robin chirped. "Do you see what I see?"

Ace checked the photo. "That's not a grandma," he said. **"That's a hyena!"**

"Exactly!" the robin shouted. "If there's a hyena in Gotham, the **Joker** is back in town."

"Dealing with that criminal clown is no laughing matter," said Ace.

Dear Master Timothy Drake

You are invited to a party

GRANNY GLE

WONDERFUL W

OF WOND

Doors open at NOON TOD

GRANNY GLEE

"Neither are his critters, **Giggles** and **Crackers**," Robin Robin added.

"To the **Batcave!**" cried Ace.

WOOOOSH!

The heroic hound and his flying friend raced to the large clock in Bruce Wayne's office. Robin Robin turned the hands on the clock's face. An entrance suddenly opened to . . . the Batcave! This chamber was the hidden headquarters of Bruce Wayne's secret identity, **Batman.**

Tim Drake was Batman's faithful sidekick, **Robin, the Boy Wonder.**

Ace and Robin Robin changed into their Super-Pet uniforms. They were going to crash the party at **Granny Glee's Wonderful World of Wonder!**

Chapter 2

DOUBLE TROUBLE

As Alfred drove through the city, Tim pressed his face against the car window. They were entering the heart of Gotham. Straight ahead stood the Wonderful World of Wonder! A long line of children snaked from the entrance to the end of the block.

"Wow!" Tim exclaimed. "Every kid in Gotham City must be here!"

Alfred stopped the car, and Tim quickly leaped out. "I won't be long," he shouted, waving goodbye.

"Take your time," replied the butler.

After a long wait, Tim finally made his way inside. The store was four levels of toys, games, and candy. The first level was an amusement park. An enormous Ferris wheel spun next to a robotic T. rex! The dino roared, to the delight of the partygoers.

On the far side of the room stood the owner, **Granny Glee.** She was smiling from ear to ear and waving happily. Tim thought he noticed four hairy paws peeking out of her lacy sleeve.

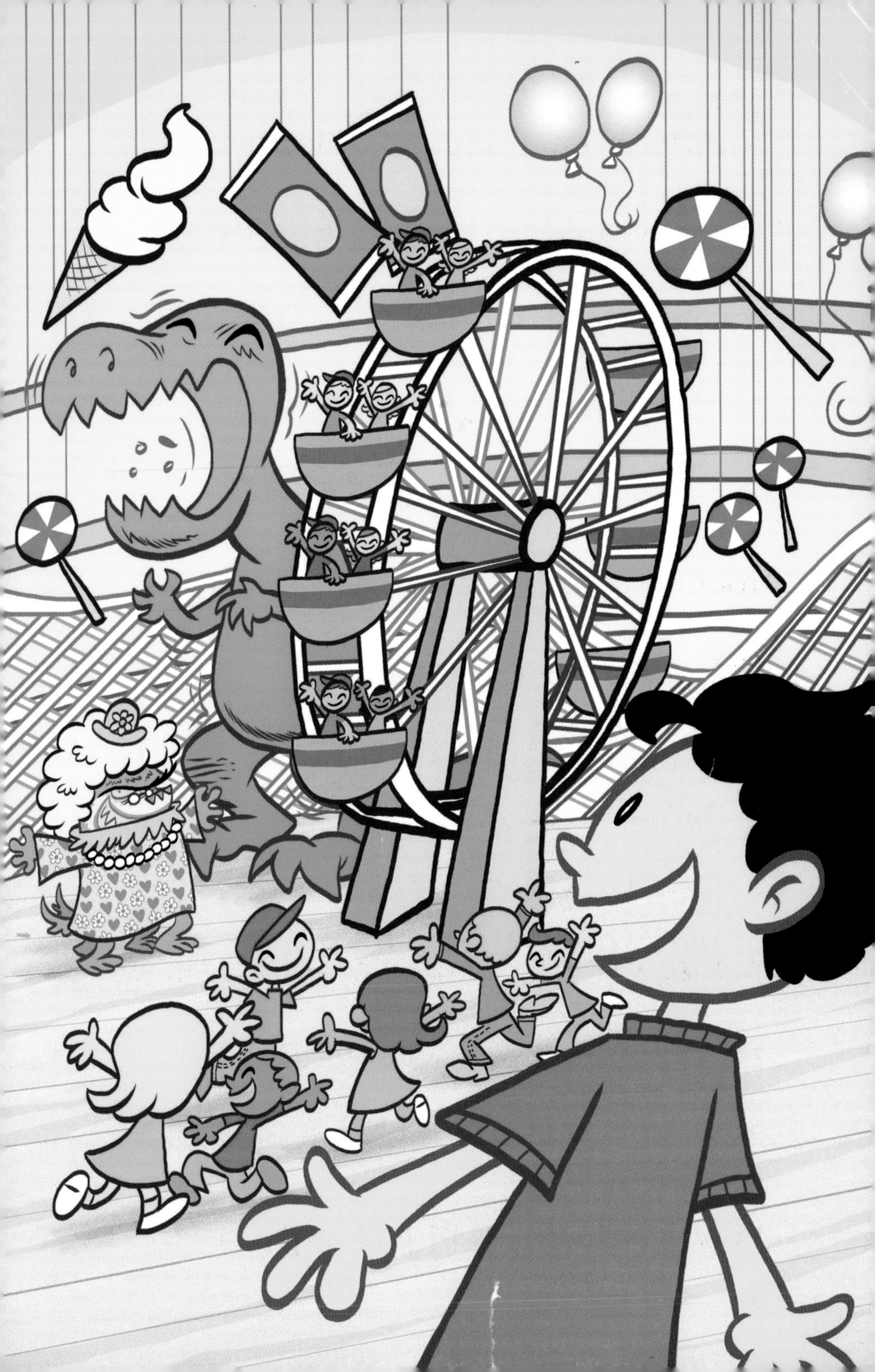

Before Tim could get a better look, a wave of children pushed him toward the ball pit. The youngsters took a running start and hopped in.

Soon, Ace and Robin Robin arrived at the party as well. The children didn't even notice as the pooch and his partner circled the room.

"I wonder what evil scheme the Joker has in mind," Robin Robin said.

Suddenly, the lights dimmed.

A spotlight shined down on a stage in the center of the room. Carnival music played through the speakers. Then the stage curtains parted, and Granny Glee stood in front of a big grinning clown head.

"Meet Happy the Hungry Clown!"

boomed a voice from the speakers.

Robin Robin thought it sounded like

the Joker's voice.

The rides suddenly came to a halt.

The lights and music stopped. "If you

want the fun to continue, you must

feed the clown," the voice said.

"What does he eat?" cried a boy.

"LUNCH MONEY!" replied the voice.

The boy jumped on stage. He

emptied his pockets into the clown's

mouth. Its big red nose lit up.

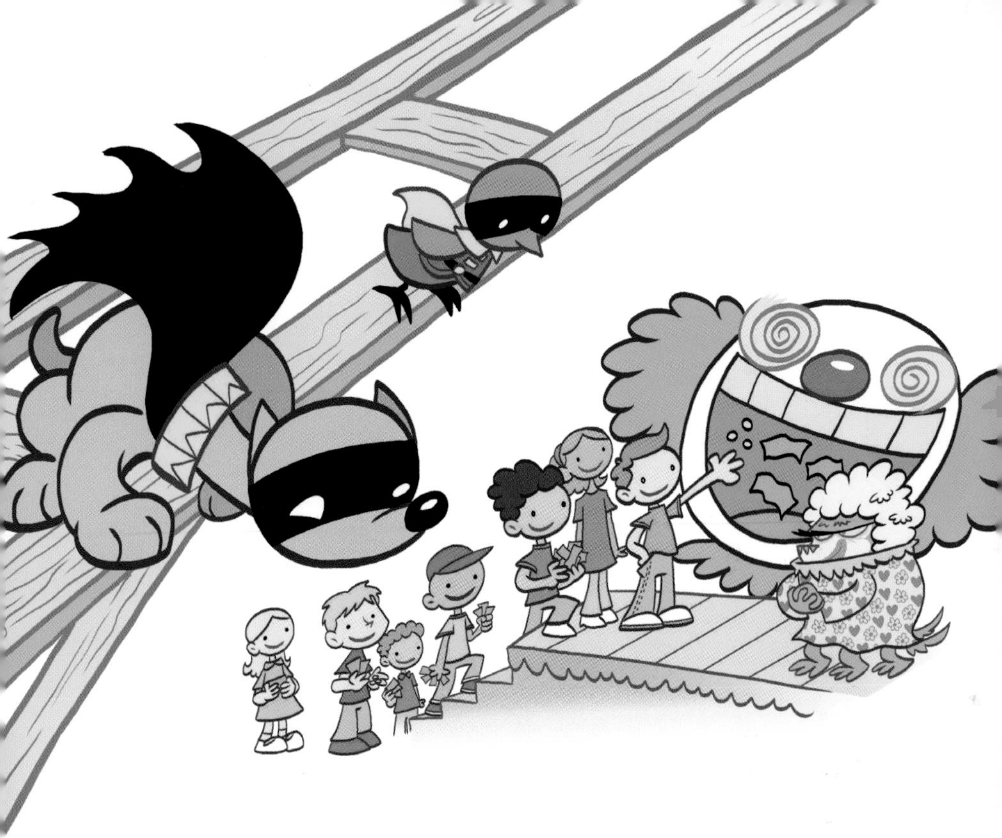

The other kids squealed with delight and ran to the stage. Each poured their money into Happy's mouth.

KA-CHING! KA-CHING!

Ace and Robin Robin had climbed onto the rafters above the stage.

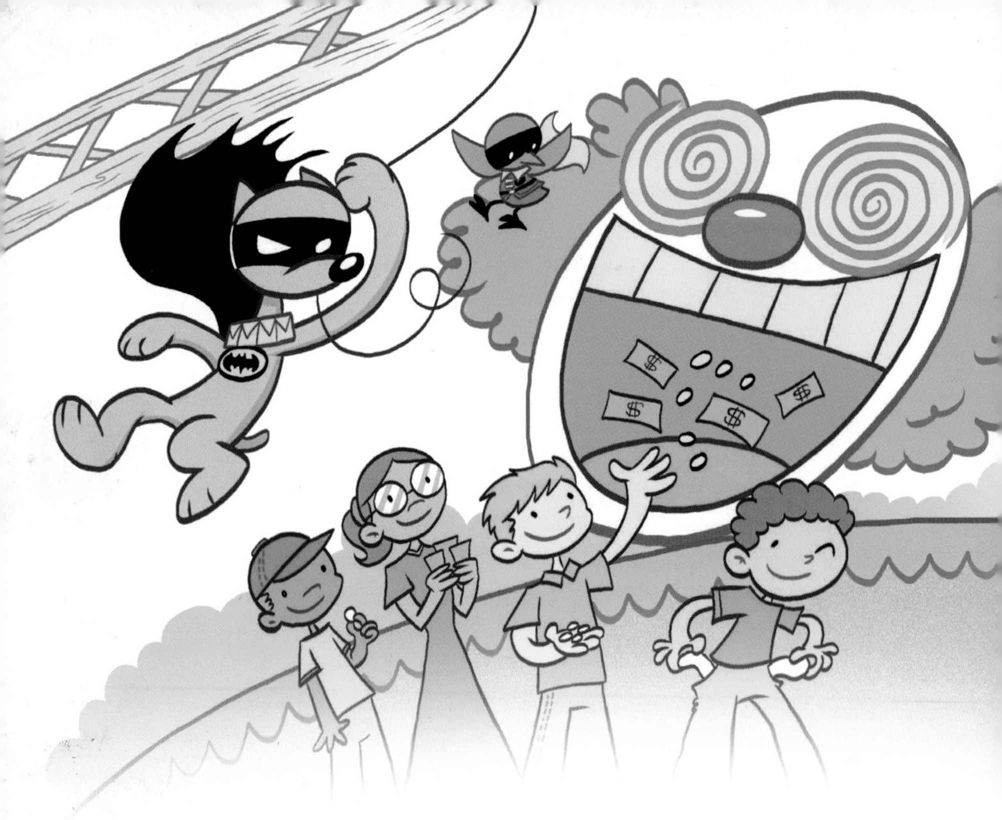

"So that's his plan," the Bat-Hound said. "He's tricking these children into giving up their allowance."

Below them, a figure moved quickly in the darkness. "I smell trouble," Ace said and leaped off the rafters.

The Bat-Hound landed in front of the figure. **It was Granny Glee!**

"My, what charming little animals you are," said the old lady sweetly. "Too bad there are no pets allowed."

Robin Robin hopped onto her shoulder. "My, what big teeth you have, Granny," he chirped.

"The better to **EAT YOU** with, my dear!" said Granny Glee.

Robin Robin flew like a flash.

He snatched Granny Glee's frilly pink hat with his little feet. Beneath it was the head of a hyena!

Ace then bit the hem of the dress with his teeth. He tore it away to find another hyena underneath. They were Crackers and Giggles, the Joker's pets.

"Looks like double trouble, Ace," Robin Robin said.

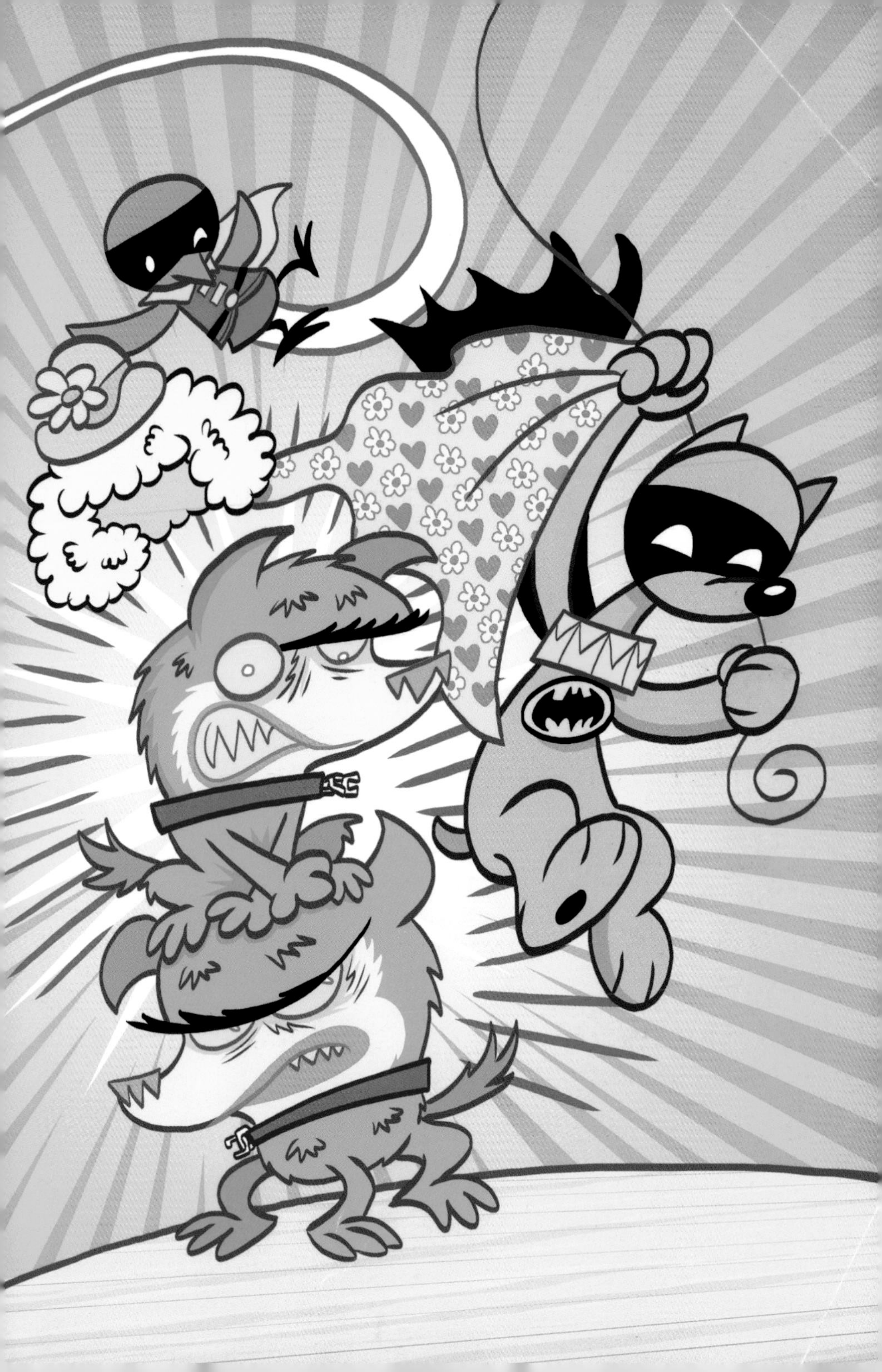

The hyenas charged onto the stage. Giggles foamed at the mouth, and Crackers cackled wildly.

At the sight of the crazed critters, the children shrieked with fear. They scrambled for the store exit.

Tim Drake climbed onto the cotton candy machine to get a better look at the stage. Ace the Bat-Hound appeared from behind the curtain. He pounced on Giggles. They wrestled around and tumbled out of sight. Robin Robin and Crackers chased after them.

"Playtime is over," Tim said to himself. **"I need to get to work."**

The super hero raced to the car where Alfred was waiting. He planned to change into his super hero uniform and return as the **Boy Wonder.**

Meanwhile, the Super-Pets faced off against their foes. Giggles wrestled Ace to the ground and laughed in his face.

"I'm going to take a bite out of crime fighting!" Giggles giggled.

"Your jokes stink worse than your breath," Ace spat back.

Giggles showed his shiny teeth. Before he could chomp down on the Caped Canine, Robin Robin flew by overhead. He carried a large peppermint candy cane in his tiny bird feet.

"Here's a hint," Robin Robin cried.
"Use a mint!" He dropped the candy
cane right onto the hyena's head.

KRAAAACK!

Giggles rubbed his throbbing

noggin. Then he scampered to the

other side of the store.

The Super-Pets gave chase, but they ran into a sneaky surprise. Crackers was waiting for them! He emptied a jar of jellybeans onto the floor. Ace lost his footing. He went slipping and sliding into a display of video game boxes.

Robin Robin flew to his friend's aid. But suddenly, Giggles scooped the tiny hero into the empty

jellybean jar and screwed on the lid.

The robin pecked against the glass. It was too strong for his beak to break.

As Ace dug his way out from the boxes, Crackers reached for a control panel on the wall.

The panel controlled the robot
dinosaur. The hyena pulled a lever,
and the T. rex lurched toward the Ace.
With another push of a button, the
dino's mouth clamped shut.

"How funny!" said Giggles. **"The dinosaur will make YOU extinct!"**

Ace was trapped inside the T. rex's jaws! He pushed against the metal teeth, but they wouldn't budge. The hero needed to think fast before his partner ran out of air.

Like his owner, Batman, Ace had a Utility Belt full of gadgets. He pulled out a pair of earplugs and stuffed his ears. Then he took out a supersonic alarm. This device made a sound strong enough to break glass.

Ace pressed the button.

BWEEEEE!

The hyenas had such sensitive

hearing that the sound sent them

running for cover.

Then, suddenly, the bottle holding Robin Robin shattered to pieces. The high-flying hero soared toward the control panel. With his little feet, Robin Robin pulled the lever.

The dinosaur's mouth flipped open. Ace was free!

"Now that's what I call **teamwork,"** the little bird said.

"But our work is far from over," said Ace. **"Let's find those laughing loons and wipe the grins off their faces."**

Chapter 3

THE LAST LAUGH

Ace sniffed the ground for the hyenas' scent. He followed it onto the candy store stage.

"The trail ends here," Ace said. He pointed to the clown's open mouth.

Together, Ace and Robin Robin jumped into Happy's head.

Behind the face was a slide leading

into the basement. The heroes swirled

until they landed with a THUMP!

The pets found themselves in a pile

of money. Nearby, a table was covered

with even more loot. The **Joker** and his

friend **Harley Quinn** were counting it.

The real Granny Glee was tied to a chair with licorice ropes. Crackers and Giggles were guarding her. Drool dripped from their fangs.

The Joker jumped from his seat. **"Doggone it!"** he cried. **"We've been found by the hound!"** The villain shoved the loot into a large sack.

Harley Quinn whistled at the hyenas. **"Get them!"** she cried.

Crackers and Giggles bounded toward the Super-Pets. **BOING!**

Suddenly, there was another loud **THUMP!** Everyone turned to see the Boy Wonder. He had found the slide and come to help the Super-Pets.

"Looks like the joke is on you," Robin said. "You're not the only one with an ace up your sleeve!"

"It's the Boy Brat!" the Joker sneered. He reached into his gag bag. "Here, pick a card . . . any card!"

The Joker threw a deck of exploding cards at the ground. Green smoke filled the room, blinding the heroes.

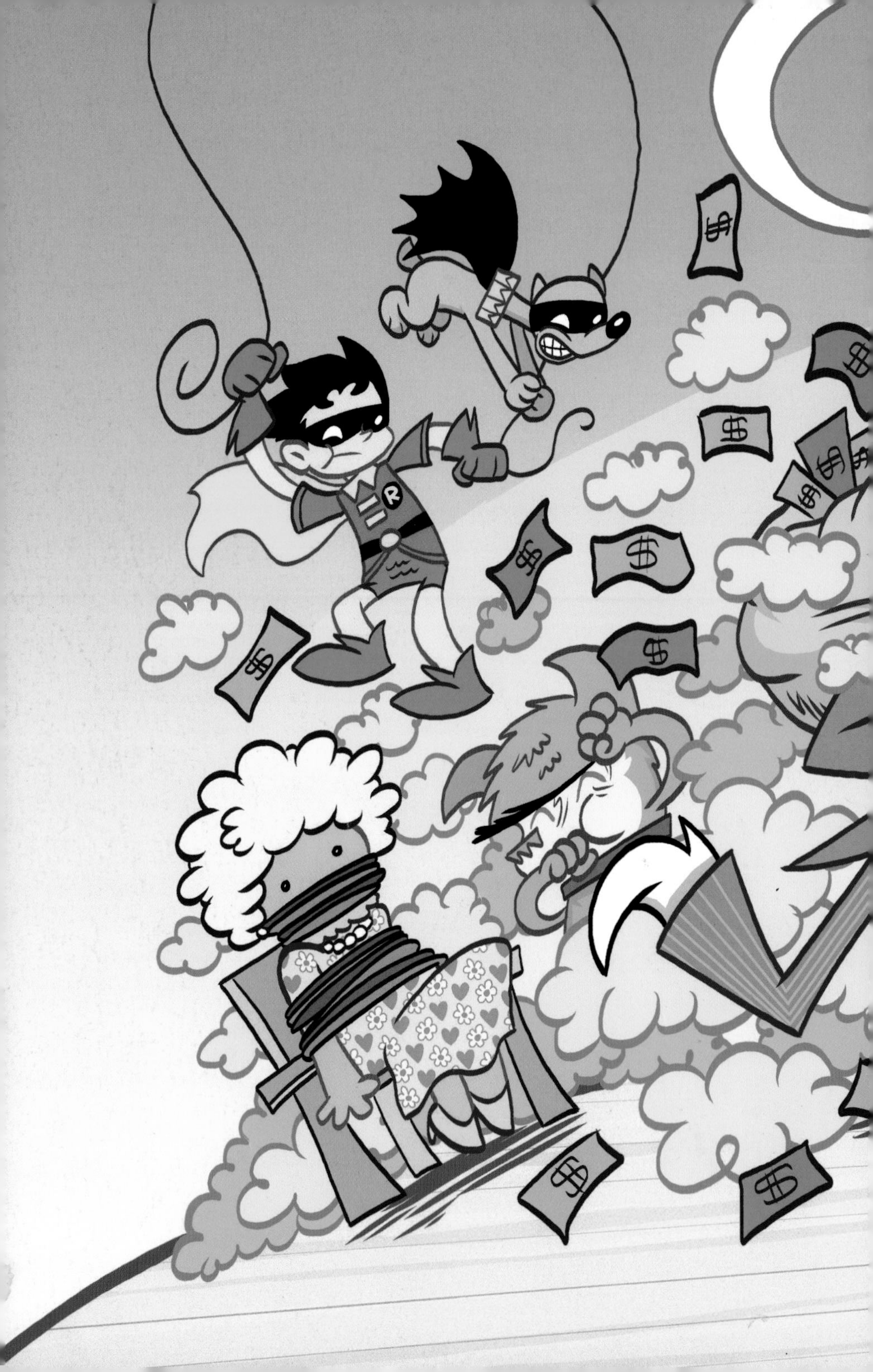

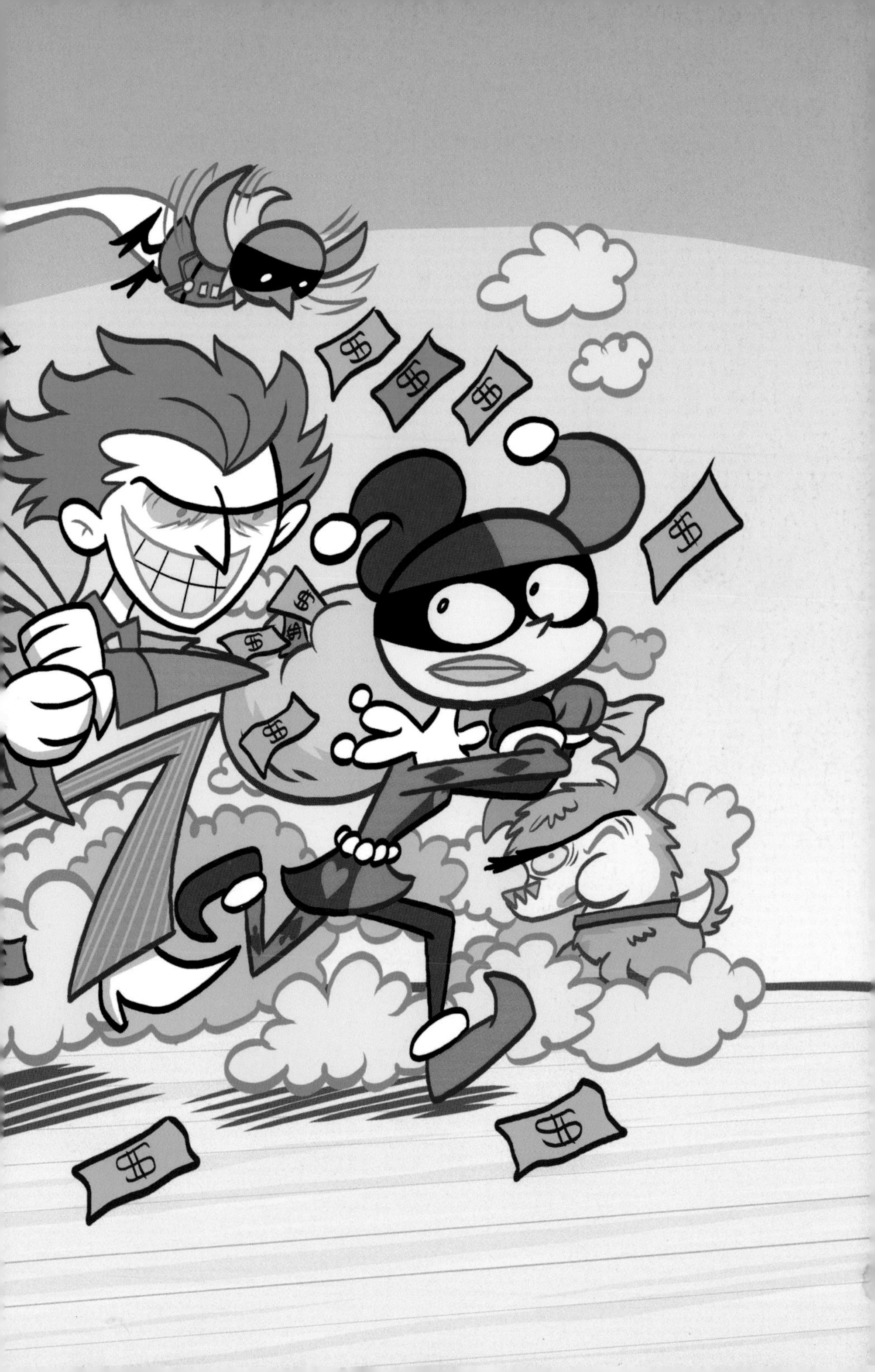

The smoke cleared. The Joker and Harley Quinn were gone, but the hyenas were still there. Robin pulled out his **Batrope.** He twirled the **Batarang** and launched it into the air.

 "Fetch!" Robin yelled to Ace. The Bat-Hound leaped over the hyenas and caught the Batarang in his teeth.

Ace and Robin ran in opposite directions. They tied the twin terrors back to back. "Sit tight," Robin said.

Ace happily chewed through Granny Glee's licorice ropes.

"Thank you, my dear," she said to

Ace, patting him on the head. Then

she turned to the Boy Wonder.

Granny Glee told the tale of how the

villains broke into her store, tied her

up, and sent out the fake invites.

"Do you know where that leads?"
Robin asked, pointing at an elevator.

"To the roof," said Granny Glee,
"where they parked their helicopter!"

The heroes ran to the elevator.
The button to call it back had been
smashed. Then Robin noticed that his
pet bird was missing. Ace pointed to a
tiny vent in the ceiling. Robin Robin
had taken a shortcut to the roof.

"Aw, yeah!" the Boy Wonder cheered
as he and Ace sprinted to the stairs.

Meanwhile, the Joker and Harley Quinn climbed into their getaway vehicle. They howled with laughter.

"This caper was as easy as stealing candy from a baby!" Harley said.

The Joker reached into his pocket and pulled out a lollipop. **"Actually, I did that, too!"** he squealed.

Just then, Robin Robin soared out of a vent on the rooftop. He carried a tiny box that he had lifted out of the Joker's gag bag — **sneezing powder!**

As the helicopter took off, Robin

Robin flung the box inside.

A cloud of powder filled the copter's

cockpit. The partners in crime sneezed

uncontrollably. **"Ah-choo! Ah-choo!"**

Joker and Harley sneezed so hard that they head-butted each other. The copter crashed back onto the rooftop.

Moments later, the door to the roof opened. Robin and Ace appeared. They pulled the crooks from the damaged copter and tied them together. Robin called **Police Commissioner Gordon.**

When the Commissioner and his officers arrived, he thanked the Boy Wonder and the Super-Pets. "Whenever Batman is away, I know Gotham City is in good hands," Gordon said.

"**And paws,**" Robin stated. **Ace**

barked in agreement.

"**And wings!**" Robin chirped.

✳   ✳   ✳

The next day, Granny Glee invited all the guests back to her Wonderful World of Wonder. All the stolen money was returned, and she let the children enjoy a free day of fun.

Tim Drake, Ace, and Robin Robin took turns riding the giant slide into the Peppermint Pool. "Ah, sweet!" said Tim. Ace barked and Robin Robin chirped happily.

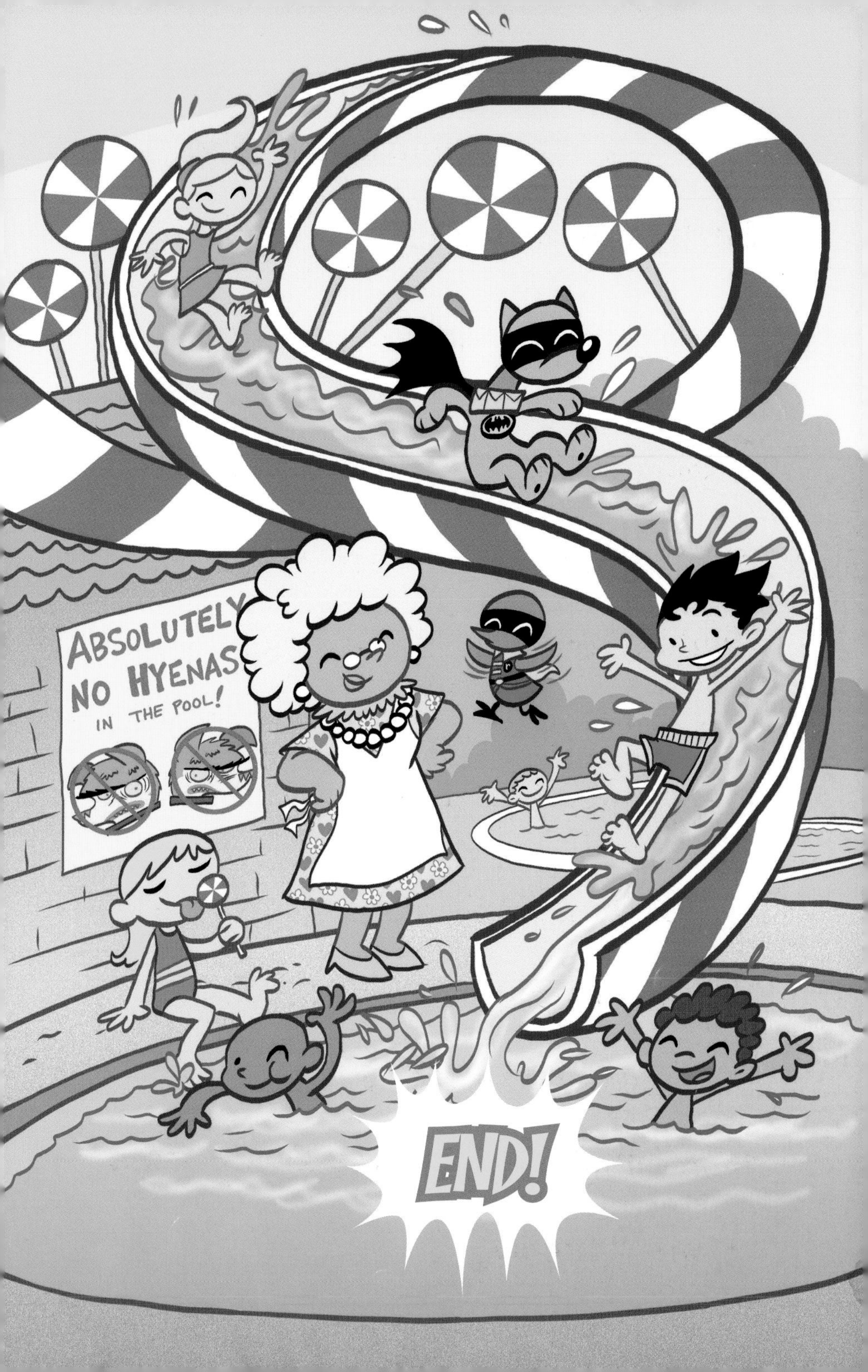
ABSOLUTELY NO HYENAS IN THE POOL!
END!

KNOW YOUR HERO PETS!

1. Krypto
2. Streaky
3. Beppo
4. Comet
5. Super-Turtle
6. Fuzzy
7. Ace
8. Robin Robin
9. Batcow
10. Jumpa
11. Whatzit
12. Hoppy
13. Storm
14. Topo
15. Ark
16. Fluffy
17. Proty
18. Gleek
19. Big Ted
20. Dawg
21. Paw Pooch
22. Bull Dog
23. Chameleon Collie
24. Hot Dog
25. Tail Terrier
26. Tusky Husky
27. Mammoth Mutt
28. Rex the Wonder Dog
29. B'dg
30. Sen-Tag
31. Fendor
32. Stripezoid
33. Zallion
34. Ribitz
35. Bzzd
36. Gratch
37. Buzzoo
38. Fossfur
39. Zhoomp
40. Eeny

1

2

3

4

5

6

7

8

9

10

11

12

13

14

15

16

17

18

19

20

21

22

23

24

25

26

27

28

29

30

31

32

33

34

35

36

37

38

39

40

KNOW YOUR VILLAIN PETS!

1. Bizarro Krypto
2. Ignatius
3. Brainicat
4. Mechanikat
5. Crackers
6. Giggles
7. Joker Fish
8. Rozz
9. Artie Puffin
10. Griff
11. Waddles
12. Mad Catter
13. Dogwood
14. Chauncey
15. Misty
16. Sneezers
17. General Manx
18. Nizz
19. Fer-El
20. Titano
21. Mr. Mind
22. Sobek
23. Bit-Bit
24. X-43
25. Starro
26. Dex-Starr
27. Glomulus
28. Rhinoldo
29. Whoosh
30. Pronto
31. Snorrt
32. Rolf
33. Squealer
34. Kajunn
35. Tootz
36. Eezix
37. Donald
38. Waxxee
39. Fimble
40. Webbik

 1
 2
 3
 4

 5
 *6*
 7
 8

 9
 10
 11
 12

 13
 14
 15
 16

 17
 18
 19
 20

 21
 22
 23
 24

 25
 26
 27
 28

 29
 30
31
32
33
34

 35
 36
 37
 38
 39
 40

MEET THE AUTHOR!

John Sazaklis

John is super lucky to have written, and sometimes illustrated, many children's books about his favorite characters. To him, it's a dream come true. He has been reading comics and watching cartoons since before even the internet! John lives with his beautiful wife, Nicoletta, in the Big Apple.

MEET THE ILLUSTRATOR!

Eisner Award-winner Art Baltazar

Art Baltazar is a cartoonist machine from the heart of Chicago! He defines cartoons and comics not only as an art style, but as a way of life. Currently, Art is the creative force behind *The New York Times* best-selling, Eisner Award-winning, DC Comics series Tiny Titans, and the co-writer for *Billy Batson and the Magic of SHAZAM!* Art is living the dream! He draws comics and never has to leave the house. He lives with his lovely wife, Rose, big boy Sonny, little boy Gordon, and little girl Audrey. Right on!

carnival (KAR-nuh-vuhl)—a public celebration, often with rides, games, and parades

chamber (CHAYM-bur)—a large room

delight (di-LITE)—great pleasure

enormous (i-NOR-muhss)—extremely large

extinct (ek-STINGKT)—no longer living

faithful (FAYTH-fuhl)—loyal and trustworthy, or sturdy and dependable

hyena (hye-EE-nuh)—a wild animal that looks somewhat like a dog. It eats meat and has a shrieking howl that sounds like laughter.

scheme (SKEEM)—a plan or plot for doing something, or to plan and plot something secret or dishonest in nature

supersonic (soo-pur-SON-ik)—faster than the speed of sound

ART BALTAZAR SAYS:

HERO DOGS
GALORE!

SPACE CANINE
PATROL AGENCY!

KRYPTO THE
SUPER-DOG!

BATCOW!

FLUFFY AND THE
AQUA-PETS!

PLASTIC
FROG!

JUMPA
THE KANGA!

STORM AND THE
AQUA-PETS!

STREAKY
THE SUPER-CAT!

THE TERRIFIC
WHATZIT!

SUPER-TURTLE!

BIG TED
AND DAWG!

Read all of these totally awesome stories today, starring all of your favorite DC SUPER-PETS!

GREEN LANTERN BUG CORPS!

SPOT!

ROBIN ROBIN AND ACE TEAM-UP!

SPACE CANINE PATROL AGENCY!

HOPPY!

BEPPO THE SUPER-MONKEY!

ACE THE BAT-HOUND!

KRYPTO AND ACE TEAM-UP!

B'DG, THE GREEN LANTERN!

THE LEGION OF SUPER-PETS!

COMET THE SUPER-HORSE!

DOWN HOME CRITTER GANG!

Picture Window Books™

Published in 2013
A Capstone Imprint
1710 Roe Crest Drive
North Mankato, MN 56003
www.mycapstone.com

Copyright © 2013 DC Comics.
DC SUPER-PETS and all related characters and
elements © & ™ DC Comics.
(s13)

STAR25285

Cataloging-in-Publication Data is available
at the Library of Congress website.
ISBN: 978-1-4048-6484-9 (library binding)
ISBN: 978-1-4048-7214-1 (paperback)

Summary: When an evil old lady opens a
candy store in Gotham, Dick Grayson and
his friends can't resist her terribly sweet
treats. Luckily, the Boy Wonder's pet, Robin
Robin, has a bird's-eye view of the sugary
scheme. But the hairy truth behind Granny's
grand plan will surprise even this early bird.

Art Director & Designer: Bob Lentz
Editor: Donald Lemke
Creative Director: Heather Kindseth
Editorial Director: Michael Dahl

Printed and bound in the USA
0482

DC SUPER-PETS!™

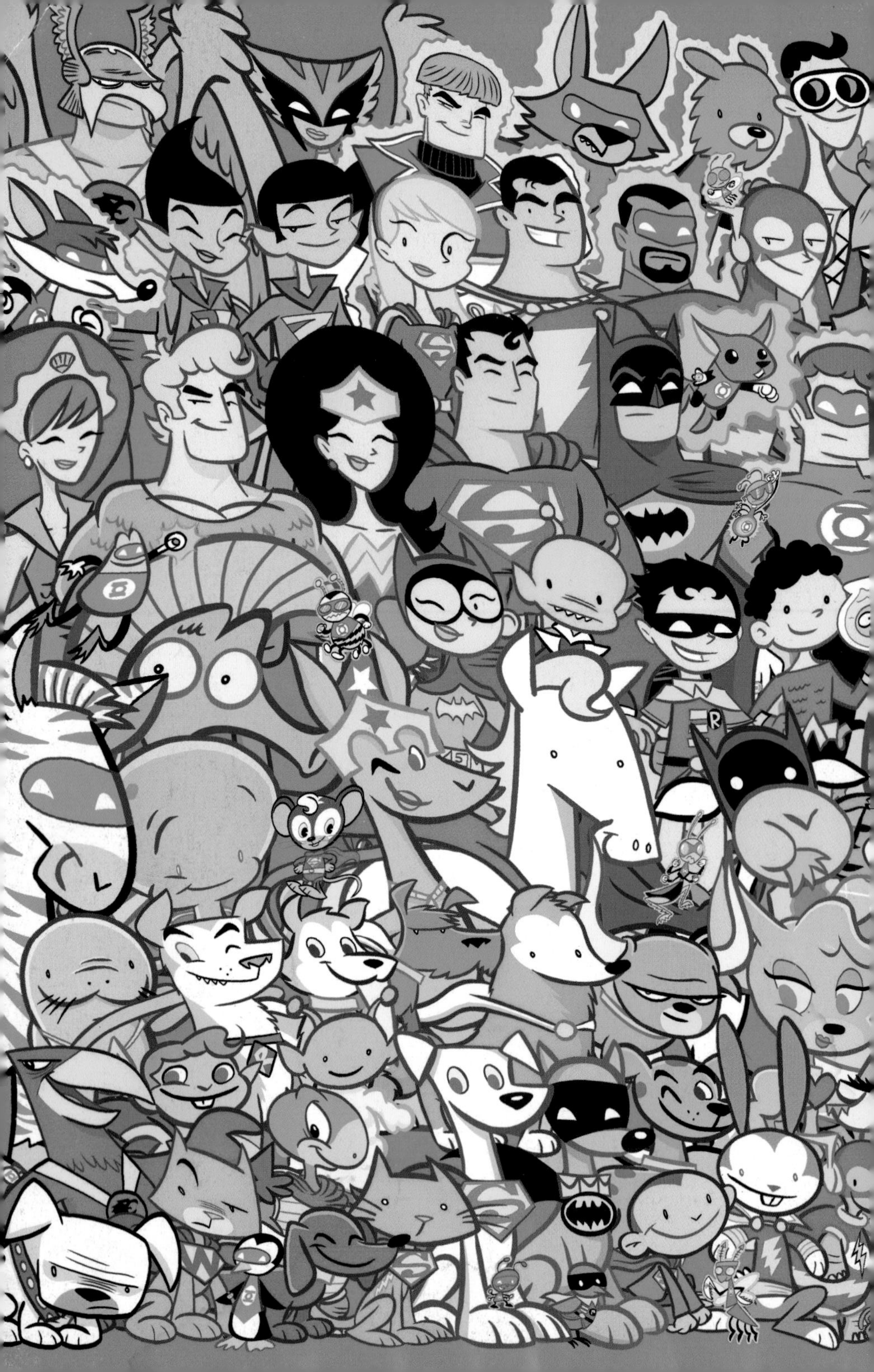

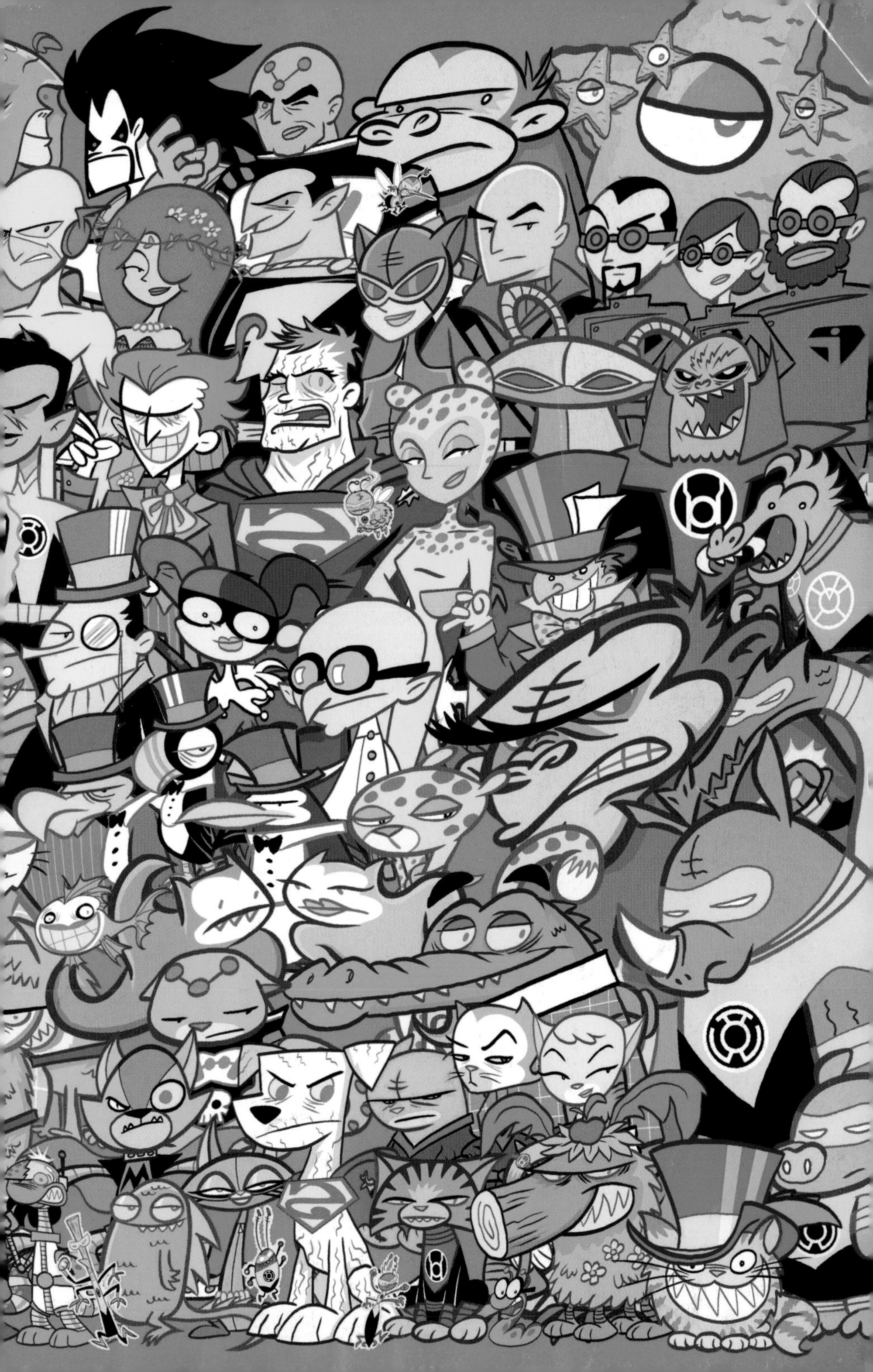

DC SUPER-PETS! ™

5

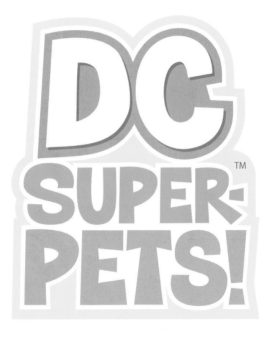